EVERYTHING IS
AWESOME

A SEARCH-AND-FIND
CELEBRATION OF
LEGO® HISTORY

Random House 🏠 New York

By Simon Beecroft
Illustrated by AMEET Studio

LEGO, the LEGO logo, the Brick and Knob configurations, the Minifigure,
DUPLO, MINDSTORMS, NINJAGO and VIDIYO are trademarks and/or copyrights
of the LEGO Group. ©2021 The LEGO Group. All rights reserved.

 Manufactured under license granted to
AMEET Sp. z o.o. by the LEGO Group.

AMEET Sp. z o.o.
Nowe Sady 6, 94–102 Łódź – Poland
ameet@ameet.eu, www.ameet.eu

www.LEGO.com

Published in the United States by Random House Children's Books, a division
of Penguin Random House LLC, 1745 Broadway, New York, NY 10019, and in
Canada by Penguin Random House Canada Limited, Toronto. Random House
and the colophon are registered trademarks of Penguin Random House LLC.

rhcbooks.com

ISBN 978-0-593-43025-5 (trade) — ISBN 978-0-593-48245-2 (ebook)

Printed in the United States of America

10 9 8 7 6 5 4 3 2 1

WELCOME TO THE AMAZING LEGO® WORLD!

Step back through time and discover all the most amazing LEGO toys ever made.

Which sets and minifigures do you recognize?
Which toys do you think are the coolest?

Each scene is packed with details and interesting characters ...

**But wait, there's more!
Head to the back of the book ...**

Building a World (1932–1969)
At first, LEGO® toys were completely made of wood. Wooden animals, vehicles, buildings and more emerged from the little Danish factory. But in the late 1940s, plastic toys and bricks arrived and the LEGO Town theme began to grow.

EXTRA THINGS TO FIND

Happy birthday ... to me!
Cake Guy celebrates 40 years of minifigures in 2018.

My wheelchair was new in 2016.
Boy in a wheelchair from LEGOLAND set.

I like to dance!
Vernie – the moving, talking robot from LEGO® Boost.

Alien from unreleased space theme, Sea-Tron.

My monkey friend is called Ingo.
Tim goes time travelling in LEGO Time Cruisers.

I'm very rare to find now!
Minifigure for Fan Weekend event in Denmark in 2009.

I help fight mischief on LEGO Island.
Stunt skateboarder Sky Lane from LEGO Island.

I co-founded LEGO Ninjago.
Tommy Andreasen works at the LEGO Group.

... and there are 10 things to search for in every scene!

**... for more special things to spot.
Now you're a real superfan!**

Try these other games and challenges!

Challenge someone to guess which minifigure you are thinking of—in 20 questions or less!

How many things can you find that start with the first letter of your name?

There's a duck in every scene. Can you spot them all?

What other games could you play?

Pick a minifigure or detail and challenge someone else to find it.

How about hunting for all the minifigures in red trousers?

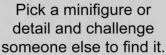

Building a World (1932–1969)

At first, LEGO® toys were completely made of wood. Wooden animals, vehicles, buildings and more emerged from the little Danish factory. But in the late 1940s, plastic toys and bricks arrived and the LEGO Town theme began to grow.

Ferguson tractor

Wooden yo-yo

Plastic fish rattle

"Halt!" police officer

Wooden bunny

Wooden duck

Stacking soldier

Saloon car

Brick-built clown

Wooden ladybird

Meet the Minifigures! (1970–1985)

Minifigures arrived in 1978 and quickly became the new kids on the block. They lived busy lives in the town and enjoyed the knight life in their castles. Even outer space was a brighter place with five different colors of astronaut!

Well-dressed shopper

DUPLO® farmer

Ernie Elephant

Roadworks tractor

DUPLO dog

Firefighter with ax

Michael Mouse

Brick-built horse

Classic spaceman

Princess

Choose Your Side! (1985–1990)

At first, townspeople, knights, and space explorers ruled the toy sets. Then, in 1989, new minifigures appeared, with scruffy beards, eye patches and peg legs—pirates! Adventures could now take place on land or sea—and always with a smile!

Captain Redbeard

Pirate with map

Governor Broadside

Blacktron astronaut

M:Tron astronaut

Chilling pirate

Space Police officer

Forestwoman

Futuron astronaut

Forestman

Fun in the Sun (1991–1995)

Slip on shades and crank up the boogie box—it's a '90s beach party! Join the fun in Paradisa, a new subtheme of Town, with its awesome pink bricks, sailboards and dolphins. Updated pirates and astronauts also arrived on the scene at this time.

Spyrius droid

Majisto the wizard

Space Police II officer

King Kahuka

Blacktron II commander

Music fan

Female islander

Dragon Master

Skeleton

Space explorer

Epic Adventures (1996–2000)

We've met knights, townspeople and other landlubbers . . . now let's dive underwater and meet the Aquazoners! In the 1990s, the action never stopped—below the waves, around the world, in the supernatural realm, and even through time and space!

Pippin Reed

Dr. Cyber

Willa the Witch

Aquashark leader

Camera operator

Stingray commander

Orange Pteranodon

Robber Chief

Arctic explorer

Villainous Slyboots

New Stories (2001–2005)

In the 2000s, fans could make LEGO® movies with LEGO Studios. Will the Martians from LEGO Space take over? Can the LEGO Alpha Team stop the evil Ogel? What adventures will the BIONICLE action figures have? You're the director!

Tahu Nuva

Ogel

Cam Attaway

Skeleton commander

Tee Vee

Centauri the Martian

Harry Potter

Viking warrior

Pepper Roni

Makuta Teridax

No Limits (2006–2010)

LEGO® EXO-FORCE™ introduced the first minifigures with rockstar haircuts! Meanwhile, LEGO Agents went on missions, LEGO® Power Miners dug underground, LEGO Hero Factory protected the galaxy, and LEGO Space Police were back!

Squidman

Meca One

REX-treme

Hikaru

Claw-Dette

Vezon

Spy Clops

Agent Trace

Doc

Eruptorr

Minifigure Crazy! (2010–present)

In 2010, a new LEGO® theme was out of the bag—collectible LEGO Minifigures! They are a quirky bunch from past and present and all walks of life. When they meet each other, the craziest things happen . . . We're looking at you, Hot Dog Man!

Hot Dog Man

Egyptian Queen

Snake Charmer

Super Wrestler

Genie

Hula Dancer

Cowboy Costume Guy

Panda Guy

Rapper

Gong and Guitar Rocker

Ninja and Friends (2011–2015)

Where will you explore today? Ninjago City, for a spot of Spinjitzu with the ninja? Heartlake City, for an adventure with LEGO® Friends? Underwater to LEGO Atlantis? Or into the land of Chima to meet the animal tribes? The action never stops!

Nya

Master Wu

Alien Commander

Cragger

Emily Jones

Lord Garmadon

Chase McCain

Lennox

Lord Vampyre

Squid Warrior

Lights, Camera, Action! (2014–2019)

The LEGO® universe burst onto the big screen in THE LEGO MOVIE™. Not to be outdone, Batman and the ninja of LEGO NINJAGO got their own movies, too. Then Emmet and friends saved the world a second time. Don't forget your popcorn!

Emmet Brickowski

Sweet Mayhem

Batman

Lord Garmadon

Vitruvius Ghost

Lord Business

The Velociraptor

The Joker

Misako

Rex Dangervest

Into the Future (2016–present)

Epic adventures are built brick by brick, and new heroes can come from anywhere. The LEGO® NEXO KNIGHTS™ protect the kingdom, while noodle delivery boy MK becomes Monkie Kid. What will you create next with your LEGO bricks?

Monkie Kid

Parker L. Jackson

Aaron Fox

Monstrox

Bag Tag Leopard

Pigsy

Macy Halbert

Monkey King

Aira Windwhistler

Hagrid

EXTRA THINGS TO FIND

Happy birthday …to me!

Cake Guy celebrates 40 years of minifigures in 2018.

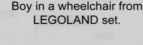
My wheelchair was new in 2016.

Boy in a wheelchair from LEGOLAND set.

I like to dance!

Vernie—the moving, talking robot from LEGO® Boost.

Alien from unreleased space theme, Sea-Tron.

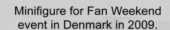
My monkey friend is called Ingo.

Tim goes time-traveling in LEGO Time Cruisers.

I'm very rare to find now!

Minifigure for Fan Weekend event in Denmark in 2009.

I help fight mischief on LEGO Island.

Stunt skateboarder Sky Lane from LEGO Island.

I co-founded LEGO Ninjago.

Tommy Andreasen works at the LEGO Group.

Honey, where are my paaants?

Larry is the star of Emmet's favorite TV show.

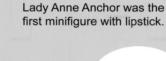
Ahoy, I'm a fearless pirate!

Lady Anne Anchor was the first minifigure with lipstick.

I battle a robot army!

Hitomi is the new leader of LEGO EXO-FORCE.

Only 5,000 of me were ever made!

Mr Gold: for the 10th series of LEGO Minifigures.

I invented the minifigure.

Jens Nygaard Knudsen was a LEGO designer.

Ninja never quit!

Shh, don't tell! Lloyd is secretly the Green Ninja.

I'm a LEGO maniac!

Zach starred in LEGO TV ads in the '80s and '90s.

I lead LEGO Adventurers!

Johnny Thunder searches the world for treasure.

This cute brown pony only appeared in Paradisa sets.

Ohmygosh ohmygosh ohmygooo—!

Robin is Batman's loud, over-excited sidekick.

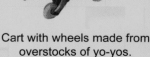
BIONICLE was one of the biggest LEGO themes ever!

Christian Faber was one of the creators of BIONICLE.

Cart with wheels made from overstocks of yo-yos.

I was a Christmas gift for the Kirk Christiansen family!

Angel made by Master Builder Dagny Holm.

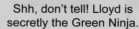

My torso sticker is unique.

The first-ever female minifigure was a doctor.

ANSWERS

Building a World

Meet the Minifigures!

Choose Your Side!

Fun in the Sun

Epic Adventures

New Stories

No Limits

Minifigure Crazy!

Ninja and Friends

Lights, Camera, Action!

Into the Future